FARM ANIMALS

TRACE TAYLOR

pig

COW

chicken

donkey

sheep

duck

goat

horse

rabbit

dog

Y/YY: Skills Card

Reader: _____ Room: _____

Benchmarks

Benchmarks	Date	Date
1. Read at home every night.		
2. Listen to and remember the title and first page.		
3. Use the title and the first page to "read" the rest of the pages.		
4. Point to each word as I read.		
5. Use the spaces to separate words.		
6. Use the picture and the first letter to figure out the words.		
7. Find my favorite page or part and tell why it is my favorite.		

I know the sound for:

b	c	d
f	g	h
j	k	l
m	n	p
r	s	t
v	w	z

Can you match the words to the pictures?

horse   chicken

sheep   goat

duck   cow